WONDER PARK

Little, Brown and Company
Hachette Book Group
1290 Avenue of the Americas, New York, NY 10104
Visit us at LBYR.com

First Edition: February 2019

LB kids is an imprint of Little, Brown and Company.
The LB kids name and logo are trademarks of Hachette Book Group, Inc.

The publisher is not responsible for websites (or their content) that are not owned by the publisher.

Library of Congress Control Number 2018956066

ISBNs: 978-0-316-44471-2 (pbk.), 978-0-316-44474-3 (ebook), 978-0-316-44473-6 (ebook), 978-0-316-44469-9 (ebook)

Printed in the United States of America

CW

10 9 8 7 6 5 4 3 2 1

Backyard Roller Coaster

Storybook adapted by Trey King

LB kids

Hey there! I'm June, and I love to build things! My mom and I used to work on this whole big amusement park!

Have you ever wanted to build something? I bet you have. Want a few pointers? Come on, there's a lot to show you!

The first thing you're going to need is a big imagination. And that's something everyone has.…You just have to look deep inside your head.

I want my amusement park to be full of all the things that make people happy. We'll definitely need a roller coaster and lots of fun stops for all the guests!

Remember: There are no bad ideas!

WONDERLAND

Now you should decide on a name for your theme park. The big one I've been working on is called Wonderland! What would you call yours?

It's time to start working on blueprints. That's a cool way of saying writing or drawing your ideas on paper. (It's my favorite part.)

Check out my design plans on the next page.

Having fun yet? You know what would be more fun? Having your friends and family work with you.

Sometimes when I can't think of new ideas, I ask other people to pitch in, too.

On my latest big project, my friend Banky has been a huge help. It's a big surprise, and I can't wait for everyone to see my...

◆◆◆ Backyard Roller Coaster!

I call it... *The Grand Wonder.*

It was a lot of work, but we put together the best ride ever before my parents were even up for breakfast. Check it out!

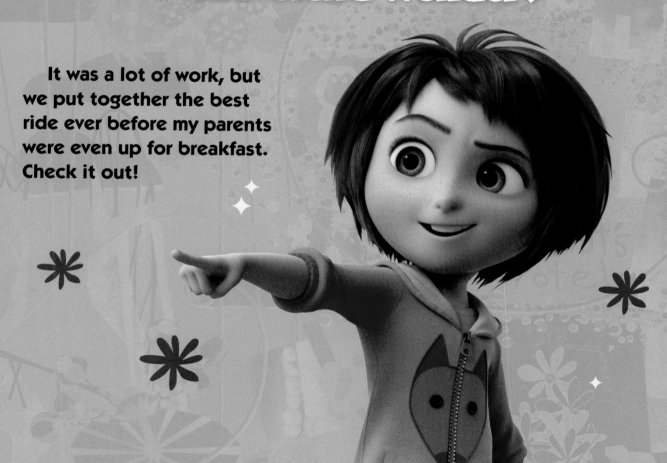

Banky is the best copilot anyone could ask for, so he gets to ride with me! But first, I've got to get the crowd excited.

"They said it couldn't be done!" I shout.
"Who said it couldn't be done?" Banky whispers.
"They."
"Who's *they*?" Banky asks.
"It's just an expression. Don't bust me on a technicality," I say to Banky.

And now, back to the crowd: "Five hundred and sixty-two feet of track. An intergalactic spaceport, complete with wormhole.

"And the *pièce de résistance*—that's French for 'super awesome'—a genuine loop-de-loop!"

GOGGLES

Oh! First things first! When you're bringing your big roller coaster dreams to life, safety is most important. Always remember to wear your goggles.

My huge moment is finally here! "Commencing test run. All systems are a go.

"Five...

four...

three...

two...

one..."

Look! It's Moon Land! WARP SPEED through the black hole!

And now we're coming up to the loop-de-loop. This is it!

OH NO! The loop isn't going to hold together! Maybe we didn't use enough tape? Maybe a screw came loose? All I know is this ride is going to get really bumpy really soon!

Another lesson we learned: When things go wrong and your track falls apart, you have to think fast!
We take a quick left turn to avoid a house, and another to avoid a bike, and a right to avoid a fence. Our neighbors sure have a lot of stuff.

The street isn't the best place for a roller coaster car still rolling at warp speed.
Especially when the brakes aren't working super well!

SCREEEEECHHHH

Yikes. We kind of ruined a lot of yards and gardens. But nobody was hurt! That's the most important thing. But we are in pretty big trouble....My parents might ground me for a while!

At least I have time to work on my Wonderland plans!
Banky is in trouble, too, but he always has fun ideas
up his sleeves.

Now for the best part: diving back into my imagination! Even when things don't go my way, I can always have fun with all my friends in Wonderland!

GRETA

STEVE

GUS & COOPER

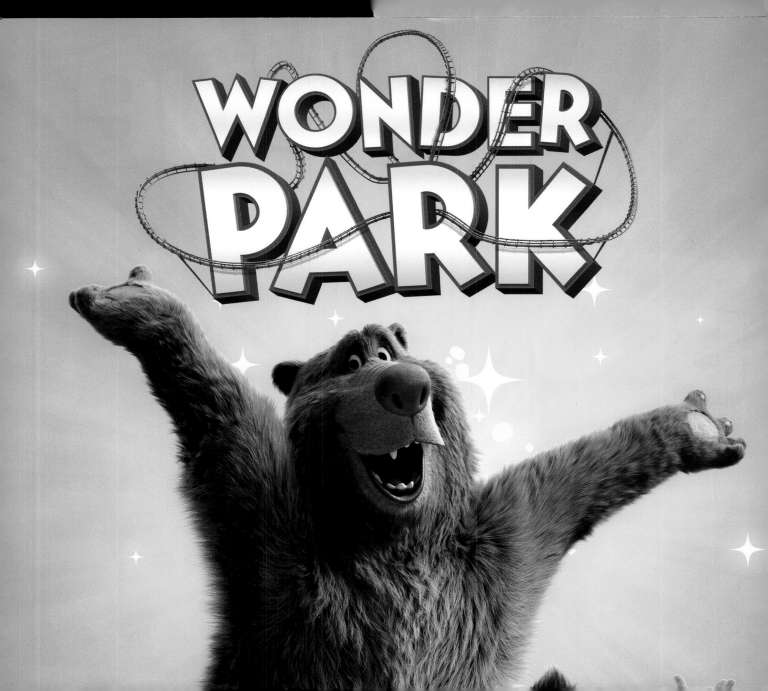